This
Book Belongs
to

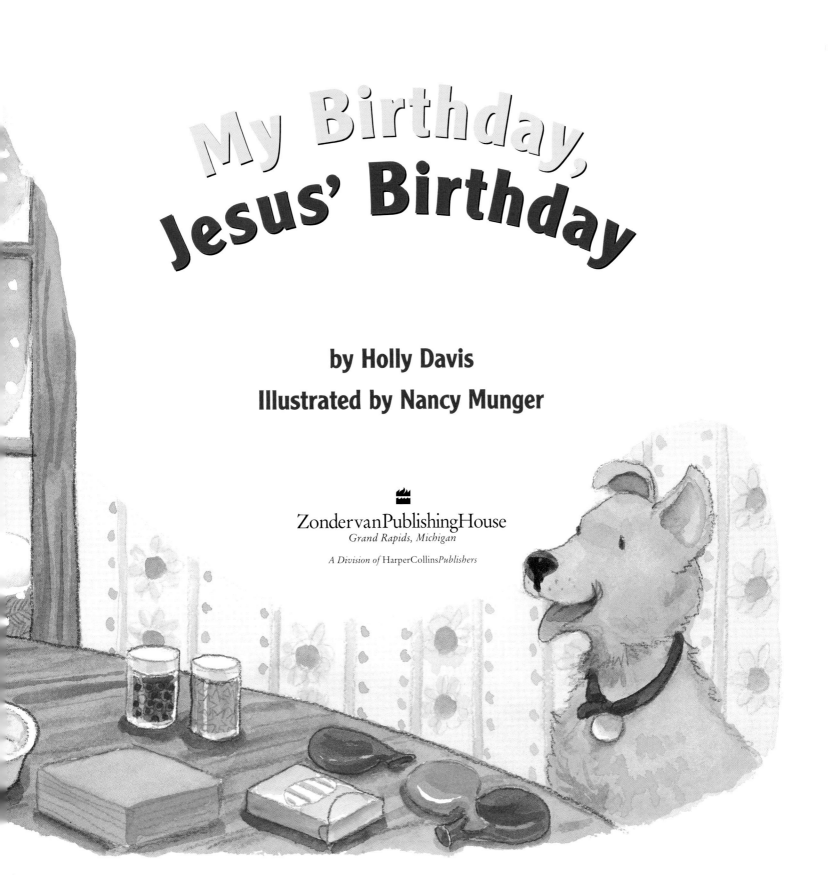

My Birthday, Jesus' Birthday

by Holly Davis

Illustrated by Nancy Munger

ZondervanPublishingHouse
Grand Rapids, Michigan
A Division of HarperCollinsPublishers

For Cassie,
who loves birthdays, Christmas, and Jesus
—H. D.

To Jessica and Joshua,
who keep me young
—N. M.

My Birthday, Jesus' Birthday
Text copyright © 1998 by Holly Davis
Illustrations copyright © 1998 by The Zondervan Corporation

Requests for information should be addressed to:

🏭 ZondervanPublishingHouse
Grand Rapids, Michigan 49530

Library of Congress Cataloging-in-Publication Data

Davis, Holly, 1952-.
    My birthday, Jesus' birthday / by Holly Davis ; illustrated by Nancy Munger.
        p.   cm.
    Summary: Compares the events surrounding a child's birth to those connected to the birth of Jesus.
    ISBN: 0-310-21968-X (hardcover)
    [1. Birthdays—Fiction. 2. Jesus Christ—Nativity—Fiction. 3. Christmas—Fiction.] I. Munger, Nancy, ill. II. Title.
PZ7.D29115Mv   1998
[E}—dc 21   98-11305
                                                                                                          CIP

This edition printed on acid-free paper and meets the American National Standards Institute Z39.48 standard.

Interior design by Sue Vandenberg Koppenol
Illustrations by Nancy Munger

Printed in China

98 99 00 01 02 03 /❖ HK/ 10 9 8 7 6 5 4 3 2 1

Every year I have two favorite days. My birthday . . . and Jesus' birthday!

My birthday is the day I was born. Everyone sings "Happy Birthday" to me. Then I blow out candles, eat chocolate cake, and open presents. I love my birthday! It's my special day.

Christmas is Jesus' birthday. My family and I sing carols to Jesus. We light candles, eat sugar cookies with sprinkles, and open presents. I love Christmas! It's Jesus' special day.

My mommy says that before I was born, God took a little of her and a little of Daddy and made me. That was my beginning!

The Bible says Jesus had no beginning. Before he was born, he lived in heaven.

9

One day, the doctor told Mommy she was going to have a baby. That baby was me!

Jesus' mother didn't need a doctor to find out she was going to have a baby. God sent an angel to tell her!

God gave me my mommy
and daddy to love me
and take care of me.

12

Jesus' father is God. But God gave Jesus a mommy and daddy to take care of him, too. Their names were Mary and Joseph.

13

Mommy and Daddy thought a long time about my name. Daddy wanted to name me after a relative. Mommy made a list of names she and Daddy liked. I'm glad they finally found the perfect name for me!

Mary and Joseph didn't have to think about names at all!
An angel told them their baby's name would be Jesus.

Before I was born, Mommy and Daddy took a long trip to visit
Grandma and Grandpa. Grandma had a warm meal and a comfy bed
ready for them when they arrived.

Before Jesus was born, Mary and Joseph took a long trip to Bethlehem. But when they arrived, they didn't have a place to stay or anyone to help them.

I was born in a hospital with doctors and nurses and baby-sized beds.
A nurse wrapped me in a blanket to keep me warm.

Jesus was born in a stable, without doctors or nurses or any beds at all. Mary wrapped Jesus in a long cloth and laid him in a manger.

When I was born, Mommy and Daddy called their family and friends to tell them the good news. Grandma and Grandpa came to the hospital to see me.

News spread about Jesus' birth, too. God sent angels to tell some shepherds, and they hurried to the stable to see Baby Jesus.

After I came home from the hospital, Mommy sent birth announcements. They were another way to let everyone know I was here.

God sent a special announcement for Jesus— a star! Wise Men from a faraway land followed the star until they found Jesus.

23

I got lots of gifts when I was born, and every birthday, I get more.
My favorite is Tum-tum, my teddy bear.

The Wise Men gave Jesus three gifts—gold, frankincense, and myrrh.

My daddy watches over me to keep me safe. He doesn't want anything bad to happen to me.

Joseph watched over Jesus—and God sent an angel to help. When bad
King Herod wanted to hurt Jesus, the angel warned Joseph to take
Jesus far away.

Sometimes I wonder what I'll be when I grow up. I can think of lots of things I'd like to be, but only God knows what will happen.

Jesus knew he was born to be a Savior. He loved us all so much, he died to save us from our sins. Then he came to life again!

The day I was born was special! Mommy and Daddy waited nine months for that day.

Jesus' birthday was special, too. People waited thousands of years for him to come! I love Jesus. I'm glad he was born to be my Savior. So every Christmas I say . . .